GEORGE WASHINGTON
and the
FIRST BALLOON FLIGHT

Story by EDMUND LINDOP
Pictures by JANE CARLSON

ALBERT WHITMAN & Company
Chicago

Boom! A cannon thundered in the cold morning air.

Boom! A second cannon blast shook the bed on which Roger Wallace and his dog, Toby, were sleeping.

Toby, nestled at the foot of the bed, sat up with a start. The frightened little black dog cocked his ears. Crawling to the head of the bed, Toby whimpered softly. Then he began to lick his master's cheek.

Roger opened his eyes and saw that the dog was trembling.

"So the cannon woke you, too?" he said gently. "Don't be frightened by those loud noises, Toby."

The boy jumped out of bed and gathered the small dog in his arms. "Quit shaking, Toby," he said as he patted him. "The cannon blasts tell us this is a special day."

But while Roger tried to calm Toby, his own heart was pounding with excitement. For this was the day when a man would climb into the basket of a balloon and try to fly into the sky.

Other men in our country had tried balloon flights, but they had all failed. Today, however, one of the world's most famous balloonists would attempt to soar high above the earth. His name was Jean Pierre Blanchard, and he had come to Philadelphia from France.

Philadelphia, where Roger lived, was an important city in the history of our country. The Declaration of Independence and the Constitution had been written in Philadelphia. And in 1790 the city became our national capital. Now, on the morning of January 9, 1793, the people of Philadelphia were looking forward to another great event.

Tickets were sold to those who wanted to be inside the courtyard where Mr. Blanchard would begin his flight. The tickets cost five dollars—a lot of money for a boy to earn. But Roger was eager to see the Frenchman take off in his balloon. He spent long hours working for his father, a cabinet maker. He ran errands for Mr. Bowen, who had a waxworks exhibition on High Street. It was at Mr. Bowen's house that the balloonist had been staying since coming to the city in December.

Roger wished Mr. Bowen would tell Mr. Blanchard that he knew a boy who would like to help him with his flight. Many, many times Roger dreamed of riding in a balloon. But he feared his dreams would never come true.

The boy saved all his money in a big jar and counted it carefully every morning. By the day of the balloon flight he had enough money for his ticket.

After scrubbing his hands and face, Roger took his best clothes from a large wardrobe cabinet. Usually these clothes were kept for Sundays, but Roger put them on proudly today. Then he brushed Toby's coat until it shone. He wanted his pet to look handsome for the important occasion.

When he was ready to leave, Roger emptied his money from the jar and put it into his pocket. Opening the front door, he rushed out into the brisk morning air with Toby trotting at his side.

As he skipped down the cobbled street, Roger thought of being a balloonist. What a thrill to go soaring up, up, up—higher than the roofs, higher than the trees, higher than the tallest steeples.

Every fifteen minutes the cannon roared twice, reminding the citizens that this was an important day. Soon the streets were crowded with people on their way to the exciting event.

Some drove in beautiful carriages with elegantly dressed footmen. Some rode on horseback. But most of the people came on foot.

Roger soon saw Mr. Bowen in the crowd and waved to him. "Good morning, sir," he called. "Is Mr. Blanchard ready?"

"He should be," Mr. Bowen answered. "I'm sure he came long before dawn to begin getting ready."

Roger smiled as he jingled the ticket money in his pocket. "It is true that President Washington will be here?" he asked.

"Yes," answered his friend. "And Mr. Blanchard won't disappoint the President. Across the ocean, in Europe, he made forty-four balloon flights. He told me there is no reason why he should fail today."

Roger's eyes were filled with excitement. "Oh, how I wish that I could go up with him."

The man looked thoughtfully at Roger. He knew the boy longed to fly in the balloon. Finally he said, "The newspapers explained it is expensive to make the hydrogen gas to fill the balloon. Mr. Blanchard can afford only enough hydrogen to keep one person in the air."

Suddenly Mr. Bowen bent down and picked up Toby. "But what would you think of Mr. Blanchard taking your dog in the balloon?" he asked.

"Take Toby!" cried Roger in amazement.

"Yes," Mr. Bowen replied. "You are too heavy, but your dog weighs only a few pounds. The balloon could probably carry him without any trouble. And to tell you a secret, I think Mr. Blanchard would be glad to have something alive for company."

"But would the trip be safe?" Roger asked. "Would I see Toby again?"

Mr. Bowen rubbed his chin thoughtfully. "There's always some danger in balloon flights, but we must have faith in Mr. Blanchard. He has taken every care in getting ready for his flight."

Roger looked at Toby nestled in Mr. Bowen's arms. Softly he patted the top of his small black head. "Toby, how do you feel about it?" he asked. "Do you want to be the first dog in Philadelphia to fly?"

"And the first American," added Mr. Bowen, with a chuckle.

Toby lifted his head and barked several times. He seemed to know that something important would soon happen to him.

The balloon was to start its flight from the courtyard of the Walnut Street Prison. A prison seems a
strange place to hold such a great event. But its courtyard was large enough to hold many people and wide
enough for the balloon to take off.

When Mr. Bowen, Roger, and Toby reached the prison gate, the street in front was crowded. All the nearby windows were filled with men, women, and children. There were people in the trees, people on the rooftops, and even one brave boy high up on a flagpole.

Inside the courtyard a brass band was playing. The gay, lively music excited Roger. But he was even more thrilled when he caught a glimpse of the famous balloonist.

Jean Pierre Blanchard was a short man, but he looked strong. He wore a handsome blue suit and a three-cornered hat with a white plume.

Carrying Toby in his arms, Mr. Bowen pushed through the crowd with Roger at his side. They walked over to the balloonist, and Roger shook hands with him. The boy's heart beat fast.

Mr. Bowen talked with the balloonist for a few minutes. Roger could not understand what they said because they spoke in French. But when his friend handed Toby over, Roger knew his little dog was going to have a great adventure.

Suddenly the band stopped playing and the cannons roared again. This time they boomed a fifteen-gun salute. That could mean only one thing. President Washington had arrived in his white coach.

Roger looked back at the prison gate. The people were cheering and clapping their hands. With head held high and shoulders erect, President Washington stepped through the gate.

Blanchard was introduced to the President, and he bowed and thanked Mr. Washington for coming to watch him. Then the Frenchman walked over to the large yellow silk balloon, now rising a few feet from the ground but held in place by strong ropes.

A basket, painted blue, was fastened beneath the balloon. It held sandbags, scientific instruments to help the balloonist on his flight, and some food.

Soon the drums began to roll and the bugles sounded. Roger watched closely as President Washington stepped forward with a paper in his hand. First he spoke to the crowd, and then his remarks were translated into French for Mr. Blanchard.

The President said the people of the United States were honored that Mr. Blanchard had come such a long distance to make a balloon flight in our country. Then President Washington wished him good luck and handed him the paper.

It was an official letter, with the seal of the President. This letter was to be shown to anyone the Frenchman might meet when his balloon landed. Since Mr. Blanchard did not speak English, the letter would explain his trip to strangers. And the President asked in the letter that all Americans help the brave airman.

When everything was ready, the Frenchman climbed into the basket, holding Toby in his arms. Then he ordered the ropes be freed, and he threw out some sandbags.

At first the balloon swayed from side to side. Roger, watching below, held his breath. Soon it straightened and started sailing upward. Within a few seconds the balloon was soaring high above the prison walls.

The band played and the cannon boomed. The airman waved a bright flag that had the Stars and Stripes on one side and the three colors of France on the other. Leaning over the side of the basket, he tipped his three-cornered hat to the crowd below. Roger thought he could hear Toby barking as the balloon climbed higher and higher.

The boy strained his eyes to follow the balloon until it was out of sight. Then, with a worried expression, he turned to Mr. Bowen. The man put his hand on the boy's shoulder. "Remember, he has had many successful flights," he said quietly.

Rising steadily, the balloon was caught in a strong breeze. Blanchard looked down and saw riders galloping their horses in the direction the balloon was flying. The horses were racing with all their might, but they were no match for the wind-driven balloon. It glided along at the rate of twenty miles an hour. Never before had anyone in America traveled so fast!

As the balloon sailed through the clouds, Blanchard felt pleased and happy. Toby, however, was frightened. At first he tried to get out of the strange basket that was bouncing in the wind. But when he looked down and saw roofs and treetops far below, he curled up on the floor and whined. Blanchard tried to talk to him in French, but Toby understood only English. Even when the balloonist gave him a friendly pat the unhappy little dog shook with fear.

Soon a flock of pigeons approached the huge yellow ball floating through the sky. As the balloon came near, the startled birds flapped their wings wildly and gave high, shrill cries. Swiftly they flew in different directions, leaving a passage for the balloon to fly through. Blanchard laughed as he watched the squawking pigeons scurry out of sight.

Checking his instruments, Blanchard figured that his balloon had reached a height of nearly six thousand feet. It had climbed over a mile into the sky! The landscape below was so far away that the Delaware River looked like a ribbon only a few inches wide.

Everything seemed to be going smoothly, so Blanchard relaxed and ate a few biscuits. Then he gave some to Toby, who was feeling better now that he had grown used to the airship.

All of a sudden danger struck! From the south a thick fog was approaching. This could mean real trouble. Blanchard would not be able to see in the fog, and the balloon might drift across New Jersey and out to sea. The airman knew that he must act quickly. He had to land the balloon before the fog blinded him.

1522155

Hurriedly he opened the valve to release some of the hydrogen. The big yellow ball began floating downward. As it drifted toward the ground, Blanchard could see below a meadow with cows and horses. He breathed a sigh of relief, for this would be a safe place to land.

Suddenly a strong gust of wind caught the balloon and carried it southward. The meadow faded into a thick forest. In another instant the balloon and its passengers would crash into the treetops!

Moving quickly, Blanchard closed the valve and began throwing the heavy sandbags over the side to make the balloon lighter. Perspiration covered his face as he looked at the tangle of sharp branches a few feet below.

Slowly the balloon began to rise again. But Blanchard knew that a great deal of the hydrogen had escaped and he could not stay in the air much longer.

The fog began swirling around the balloon. Blanchard could hardly see the land below. But between the waves of fog he caught a glimpse of a small clearing in the forest. Hurriedly he opened the valve again and hoped the balloon would land in the clearing. Holding his breath, he clung tightly to the side of the basket. The bobbing balloon dipped dangerously near the outstretched branches. But it finally came to rest on the patch of grassland.

Toby jumped up and down and wagged his tail to show how happy he was to be back on the ground. Blanchard lifted him over the side of the basket, and the little dog ran quickly to drink water from a nearby pool.

But the balloonist's troubles were far from over. Hearing a rustle behind him, he turned around quickly. From behind a clump of trees a farmer was staring at him. Blanchard called to him in French, but the startled farmer backed away.

The airman smiled at the frightened farmer, but he knew how the poor man felt. To spy a large yellow ball dropping out of the sky was enough to frighten anyone. And when the ball collapsed into a silk bag, the farmer probably thought that this was some kind of magic.

Blanchard wanted the farmer to help him, so he showed him the letter from the President. But this did no good, for the man could not read.

A few minutes later a hunter, armed with a gun, appeared at the clearing. He was so amazed to see a huge yellow bag in the forest that he dropped his gun and lifted his hands toward heaven.

Blanchard was lost, and the men who had seen him were too frightened to help him. But within a short time two men and two women arrived on horseback. When they read the President's letter they were eager to help the stranded balloonist.

One man who spoke French told Blanchard he had landed in New Jersey at a place about fifteen miles from Philadelphia. Then the men carried the basket and the balloon to a farmhouse, where they loaded it on a cart.

Blanchard and Toby started back to Philadelphia. They traveled by horseback and carriage. It took them six hours, although they stopped for dinner, to cover the same distance they had flown in less than an hour.

Meanwhile, as the evening shadows darkened, Roger grew more concerned about Toby. He paced back and forth in front of the Bowen house. Every time a carriage or wagon approached, he looked for the white plume of the Frenchman's hat.

When the airman finally arrived, Roger rushed to greet him. Toby leaped from the carriage and bounded up to his master. Gathering the dog in his arms, the boy held him tightly.

"How does it feel to fly like a bird?" he exclaimed. "The next time you go up in a balloon, I'm going too."

That same night Mr. Blanchard went to George Washington's home to report on his trip to the President. The Frenchman thanked President Washington for his letter, explaining that it had helped him return safely. This was the first letter in America to be sent by air.

Before leaving, Mr. Blanchard gave the flag he had carried to President Washington. The President gratefully accepted it. He said, "This flag, with the colors of France on one side and the United States on the other side, tells of the strong friendship between your people and mine. It will always remind us that a Frenchman made the first successful balloon flight in America."

Independence H